Ambulance!
Robina Beckles Willson

Illustrated by
Peter Kavanagh

CORGI PUPS

AMBULANCE!
A CORGI PUPS BOOK : 0 552 546291

PRINTING HISTORY
Corgi Pups edition published 1996
Reissued in 1999

3 5 7 9 10 8 6 4

Copyright © 1996 by Robina Beckles Willson
Illustrations copyright © 1996 by Peter Kavanagh
Cover illustration by Nick Sharratt

The right of Robina Beckles Willson to be identified as the author of this work
has been asserted in accordance with the Copyright, Designs and Patents Act 1988.

Condition of Sale
This book is sold subject to the condition that it shall not, by way of trade
or otherwise, be lent, re-sold, hired out or otherwise circulated without the
publisher's prior consent in any form of binding or cover other than that in
which it is published and without a similar condition including this
condition being imposed on the subsequent purchaser.

Set in Bembo Schoolbook

Corgi Pups Books are published by Transworld Publishers,
61–63 Uxbridge Road, Ealing, London W5 5SA,
a division of The Random House Group Ltd,
in Australia by Random House Australia (Pty) Ltd,
20 Alfred Street, Milsons Point, Sydney, NSW 2061, Australia,
in New Zealand by Rnadom House New Zealand Ltd,
18 Poland Road, Glenfield, Auckland 10, New Zealand
and in South Africa by Random House (Pty) Ltd,
Endulini, 5a Jubilee Road, Parktown 2193, South Africa

Printed and bound in Great Britain by
Cox & Wyman Ltd, Reading, Berkshire.

CAVAN COUNTY LIBRARY
ACC. No. 2/137944
CLASS No. J
INVOICE NO. 5352 IES
PRICE €4.87

17 JUL 2003

CONTENTS

Chapter One   5

Chapter Two   25

Chapter Three   55

Series Reading Consultant: Prue Goodwin
Reading and Language Information Centre,
University of Reading

CHAPTER ONE

Dan was bumped and bruised,
but he did not care. He had been
one of the last to leave Birch Hill.
His dustbin bag had made a
marvellous sledge down the icy
field. On the long walk home he
thought longingly of a huge
plate of eggs, beans and chips.

As he kicked snow off his wellies, he looked into the kitchen and saw that the table was bare.

Inside Dan noticed warmth, but no smell of cooking. Then he heard his mum speaking in the hall.

Dan's hollow tummy seemed to drop down inside him as he stood listening.

"Is our baby coming *now*?" he asked his mum.

"Well, not this minute! I was trying to get the midwife, but she's out seeing someone else."

"Then I'll ring for an ambulance," said Dan firmly. "Dad told me to look after you and the baby while he was away."

"All right," said Mum, sitting down. "I'm sorry, I haven't even started your tea."

"Don't worry about tea," said Dan. "What's the number to ring?"

hos pi tal

He took her hospital card and dialled the number.

"Emergency service. Can I help you?" asked a voice.

"My mum's having a baby, and it's started," said Dan. "Please can you send us an ambulance?" He gave their name and address.

"No street name?"

"We're called Last Cottage because we're at the very end, outside the village," explained Dan.

"They'll find you," said the voice. "Has your mum got help?"

"She's got me," said Dan proudly, and he put the phone down.

"I'm glad you're home," said Mum. "How did you get on?"

"There were thousands of people, sliding on all sorts of things for sledges: trays, even a wok and a roof rack. It seems so quiet here after all that noise."

"Yes, I wish we had neighbours nearer. When the ambulance comes, we'll ask them to drop you at Mrs Field's."

"*I'm* taking you to hospital," Dan told her. "And I'm making tea."

Mum said she wasn't hungry and seemed glad to sit still while Dan cut chunks of bread, managed to burn the toast and made the baked beans only luke-warm.

But he was so hungry, he ate them in a flash. And as Mum didn't want tea, he treated himself to a can of Coke.

"My bag's upstairs by our bed. Would you like to get it? Then we'll be ready," said Mum.

Dan was halfway up the stairs when the lights went out. He felt his way to the top in pitch black and, edging round their bed, found the bag. "Take care on the stairs," called his mum. "We don't want two for the ambulance.

What a night to have a power cut.
It's a terrible weather forecast.
Blizzards!"

Dan lit a candle, and Mum sat
waiting. "You'd better put your
thickest sweater on," she said;
"gloves, boots, and that woolly
cap. It'll be freezing out there."

"Dark, too," said Dan, looking out of the window. "Do you think they'll find us? We won't show up much with a candle."

"That's true," Mum agreed. "Perhaps you'd better go outside with Dad's torch."

Dan began to send wide beams of light up the lane. At last he saw a vehicle with a flashing blue light and slithered towards it, the torchlight dipping wildly. He almost skidded into the white ambulance, which hardly showed against the snow.

"Steady now. We don't want to knock you over," said a man through the window he'd opened.

"I was just so pleased to see you," Dan told him.

"You're Mrs Tucker's boy?"

"Yes, I'm Dan. My mum's indoors," Dan replied.

"I'm Jack. I'll come and get her while my mate turns round, if he can dodge that drift. On your own, are you?" he asked as they went inside.

"My dad's away, and our nearest neighbour's out. We weren't expecting the baby yet."

"Are you well wrapped up, the both of you? It's bitter out there, though we haven't far to go – just up the motorway to the hospital. Take it easy now, Mrs Tucker. You can have a nice lie-down in the ambulance."

Dan locked up then followed his mum and Jack down the path. As he helped Mum inside, Jack said to Dan:

You go in the front with the driver if you like. Tell us the way to go!

Dan climbed into the front of the ambulance, hoping that they would drive fast. "I'm Dan," he said.

"And I'm Fred. Warm enough for you?"

"It's freezing!"
"Don't you like the snow?"
"I did this afternoon," Dan replied, and told him about Birch Hill.

"We've been busy all day with accidents." Fred drove slowly towards the motorway. There were groups of lorries sheltering under the fly-over.

"*They're* not going anywhere tonight."

"Do you think the drivers are inside?" asked Dan.

"Don't know. But *that* explains why they are there," said Fred, stopping by a police car and a ROAD CLOSED sign at the entry to the motorway. "That was our quickest way. Those lorries are stranded."

CHAPTER TWO

Dan's tummy lurched more than when he slid down Birch Hill, Fred sounded so grim.

A policeman wearing a padded jacket came and spoke at their window:

"Are you heading for the hospital? We've just had to shut this section because a jack-knifed lorry is blocking the road. We've no idea when we'll be able to re-open."

"What's best then?" asked Fred.
"You could try the road over the hill to the town. The snow is thick, but they've had snow ploughs out today."

He looked at Dan. "What are you doing out on a night like this?"

"Taking my mum to hospital. I know the way, because it's my school bus route."

"Good luck then," said the policeman, and they set off again.

Dan glanced round. Mum was
lying down with her eyes closed.
Jack was sitting by her.

"Is she OK?" he asked Fred.

"She's fine. My mate knows all
about babies. He's delivered one
or two in his time."

"I think my mum would rather be in hospital," said Dan.

"Don't you worry. We'll have her there shortly. We could try your Birch Hill."

They drove on past empty vehicles and unlit houses.

A truck
was trying to crawl
up the hill. Before he
was halfway up he gave
a loud wailing toot and
began backing down. Their
ambulance had to do the same.

"That's no go then," said Fred.
"Can't get a grip."

While the truck was turning round, they waited with their engine running, and a farmer came out from his yard, where he'd been watching them.

"You'll not get out of this valley tonight," he said to Fred, "that's for sure."

"But we've got to get to the hospital," protested Dan as they moved off cautiously. "What about the road over the moors?"

"It could be even deeper up there unless the snow plough's been through. But it's our last chance. Can you help me to find the way? Don't want us lost."

"Yes, we have picnics here in the summer," said Dan; "and this is really a road, not a little lane."

"Someone's been along first
and made a track. We're not
beaten yet," said Fred, grinding
his way through snow towards a
queue of cars.

"Look, all those cars have got here," said Dan. "Though they are standing still," he added flatly.

Cars tried to move over to let the ambulance pass them, but as Fred pulled out his wheels spun, squeaking on the softer snow. Other drivers got out of their cars and tried to push the ambulance forward, skidding on the snow.

Dan jumped down and began
digging furiously with Fred's
shovel where a front wheel was
stuck.

"Keep clear, Dan, or you'll get
hurt," shouted Fred.

They still could not shift the
ambulance.

Then they heard a noisy
engine, and a tractor with huge
tyres churned through the snow
in front of the ambulance.

Dan helped the driver to fasten
a rope between them and heave
the ambulance forward to the top
of the queue before turning back.

Now they could see why the line of cars was not moving. Although a passage had been ploughed through the drifts ahead, a lorry was blocking the entry. Dan got out again to find out what was happening, and talked to the lorry driver, who was called Derek.

A JCB was lighting the scene
with giant headlights.

"He's trying to shunt my lorry
over, out of the way," explained
Derek. "Then we'll get your
ambulance through."

"Good," said Dan. "My mum's
in there."

"Watch out!" shouted the JCB
driver, swinging the JCB's bucket
arm out to push at the lorry. His
engine roared as the lorry slowly
shifted over the snow.

"I wish I was up there in his cab. It's even better than an ambulance," thought Dan. The driver smiled triumphantly as the way was cleared, and he raised the vast arm again.

"All clear now," reported Dan, getting into the ambulance again.

"That's as may be," said Fred. "Perhaps we should send you down there with a red flag to make sure! Don't want to get stuck."

"It's a village street, then down to the valley," said Dan. "Why don't we siren our way through?"

"Risky. It could be blocked further down."

"Or someone might be driving up," added Jack, coming to look over their shoulders.

"I'll go and find out," said Dan, and jumped out again before anyone could stop him.

"There's no holding that boy," said Jack, shaking his head.

"What's up, son?" asked Derek, standing huddled by his lorry.

"I'm going to see if it's clear ahead for our ambulance," said Dan.

"Not on your own, you're not. I'm coming with you."

Dan was glad to have company as they walked into the passage which the snow plough had carved, through drifts taller than him.

The snow was so white in the moonlight that it made his eyes hurt.

Some cars were completely
buried. Hedges were mounds in
front of dark houses, only
occasionally lit by candle flickers.

There was no sound except for
their footsteps crunching on snow.

"Could be on the moon," grunted Derek. "Not a soul about. Wish I was in bed. Can see myself out in this all night."

"We mustn't be. We're taking my mum to the hospital to have a baby," Dan told him.

"Oh, we'll get *you* through. But my lorry's broken down. I won't get any help till morning."

They plodded along the slippery track. At last the road sloped down to the next valley, where they could see a long line of cars. Dan began to hurry.

"Easy now, lad. Take it steady."

They reached the cars and Dan asked: "Could you wait down here, please, while we drive through?"

"The lad's come from an ambulance, taking his mum to hospital."

"We're on top of the hill, a whole lot of us," Dan went on. "And I've walked down to see if it was safe for us to come through, so that we wouldn't get stuck in a drift, or bash into you either. Can we come down first?"

"Shall we say ten vehicles down? Then you send ten up the hill?" asked Derek.

"All right," said one man. "We've been on the road for hours. A bit longer won't hurt. And none of us thought of walking up to the top in this stuff."

"You'll count ten?" Dan asked.

"I think we'll manage that."
The driver of the first car smiled
at his anxious face.

Dan and Derek set off again. It
started to snow and blow so that
the walk was hard going.
Suddenly Derek stumbled,
swearing under his breath.

"Are you OK?" Dan asked in alarm.

"I've hurt my ankle, twisted it or something."

"Can you walk?"

"Yes, I can hobble along, but I'll be slow. You'd better go ahead. I'm holding you up. Get back to your mum now, and I'll see you lead the line through."

CHAPTER THREE

Dan couldn't admit that he was scared, going on by himself. "OK."

He just wished that he had brought Dad's torch with him. His hands and feet were aching with cold as he trudged up the hill through swirling snowflakes.

As he glanced down a side lane, he froze with fright. A giant dragon was looking towards him, his scaly tail curled out.

Dan swerved to run away, and fell into a deep drift of snow, face downwards. For a second he thought he was drowning in snow.

Then he struggled up, wiping his face with a sleeve.

When he dared to look again, Dan realized that the dragon, though twice as tall as him, was only snow. But now he could hardly see through eyes half closed against the driving snowflakes, and he jumped with terror at a row of ghosts ahead.

"Is this the way? Yes, the dragon was on my right when I fell," he told himself. And, to his relief, as he crept near, the ghosts became tall shrubs, wrapped in sack-cloth.

Only that afternoon, the snow had been exciting. Now he longed to escape. Just as he made out car lights, Fred came down the track.

"Where's that driver? Why did he let you come back on your own?" he demanded.

Dan explained and asked: "Is Mum OK?"

"She's doing fine, but she was cross we let you go off down the hill."

"She couldn't have stopped me," said Dan, though he climbed gratefully into the shelter of the ambulance.

They counted the first ten vehicles, left a message about Derek and set off through the passage. This time, even crawling along, the journey seemed quick. When they passed the cars in the valley, they gave them a welcoming chorus of toots.

"Go on. Please sound our siren," Dan urged.

Fred gave a short trill as they passed the last car and came to clearer roads with much less snow. There was little traffic, and Fred only used the siren once again, at traffic lights.

At the hospital Mum was carried inside on a stretcher. Dan found himself rocking on his feet, as Mum waved and said: "Thank you, Dan," and Fred added: "We wouldn't have made it without you, lad."

The hospital was so warm, Dan meant to take his hat and coat off before he sat down.

The next thing he knew, a nurse was smiling at him.

"Good morning, Dan," she said. "Would you like to come and see your mum and baby sister? They're both fine."

"Yes, please," said Dan. "And then I must ring my dad to tell him that I did look after Mum."

CAVAN COUNTY LIBRARY

THE END